STANLEY AND THE MAGIC LAMP

and

STANLEY'S CHRISTMAS ADVENTURE

Read all of
Stanley Lambchop's adventures

by Jeff Brown

EGMONT

STANLEY

AND THE MAGIC LAMP

and

STANLEY'S

CHRISTMAS ADVENTURE

by Jeff Brown

Pictures by Scott Nash

EGMONT

Stanley and the Magic Lamp
For Elizabeth Tobin

Stanley's Christmas Adventure
For Duncan

EGMONT
We bring stories to life

This edition published 2007
by Egmont UK Limited
239 Kensington High Street
London W8 6SA

Text copyright *Stanley and the Magic Lamp* © 1985 Jeff Brown
Text copyright *Stanley's Christmas Adventure* © 1993 Jeff Brown
Illustration copyright © 2003 Scott Nash

ISBN 978 1 4052 3037 7

1 3 5 7 9 10 8 6 4 2

www.egmont.co.uk

A CIP catalogue record for this title is available from the British Library

Typeset by Avon DataSet Ltd, Bidford on Avon, Warwickshire
Printed and bound in Great Britain by the CPI Group

STANLEY
AND THE
MAGIC LAMP

by Jeff Brown

Pictures by Scott Nash

EGMONT

CONTENTS

Prologue

Once upon a very long time ago, way before the beginning of today's sort of people, there was a magical kingdom in which everyone lived forever, and anyone of importance was a genie, mostly the friendly kind. The few wicked genies kept out of sight in mountain caves or at the bottoms of rivers. They had no wish to provoke the great Genie King, who ruled very comfortably from an enormous palace with many towers and courtyards, and gardens with reflecting pools.

The Genie King took a special interest in the genie princes of the kingdom, and was noted for his patience with their high spirits and desire for adventure. The Genie Queen, in fact, thought he was *too* patient with them, and she said so one morning in the throne room, where the King was studying reports and proposals for new magic spells.

'Training, that's what they need. Discipline!' She adjusted the Magic Mirror on the throne-room wall. 'Florts and collibots! Granting wishes, which is what they'll be doing one day, is serious work.'

'Florts yourself! You're too hard on these lads,' said the Genie King, and then he frowned. 'This report here, though, says that one of them has been behaving very badly indeed.'

'Haraz, right?' said the Queen. 'He's the worst. What a smarty!'

The Genie King sent a thought to summon Prince Haraz, which is all such a ruler has to do when he wants somebody, and a moment later the young genie flew into the throne room, did a triple flip, and hovered in the air before the throne.

'That's no way to present yourself!' The Queen was furious. 'Really!'

Prince Haraz grinned. 'What's up?'

'You are!' said the King. 'Come down here!'

'No problem,' said the Prince, landing.

'It seems you have been playing a great many magical jokes,' said the King, tapping the reports before him. 'Very *annoying* jokes, such as causing the army's carpets to fly only in circles, which made all my soldiers dizzy.'

'That was a good one!' laughed the Prince.

'And turning the Chief Wizard's wand into a sausage while he was casting a major spell, you did that?'

'Ha, ha! You should have seen his face!' said the Prince.

'Stop laughing!' cried the Queen. 'Oh, this is shameful! You should be heavily punished!'

'He's just a boy, dear, only two hundred years old,' said the King. 'But I'll –'

'Who knows what *more* he's done?' said the Queen, turning to the Magic Mirror. 'Magic Mirror, what other silly jokes has this fellow played!'

The Magic Mirror squirted apple juice all over her face and the front of her dress.

'Oooooohh!' The Queen whirled around.

'Florts and collibots! I know who's responsible for *that*!'

Prince Haraz blushed and tried to look sorry, but it was too late.

'That does it!' said the Genie King. 'Lamp duty for you, you rascal! One thousand years of service to a lamp.' He turned to the Queen. 'How's that, my dear?'

'Make it two thousand,' said the Queen, drying her face.

Chapter One

Prince Haraz

Almost a year had passed since Stanley Lambchop got over being flat, which he had become when his big bulletin board settled on him during the night. It had been a pleasant, restful time for all the Lambchops, as this particular evening was.

Dinner was over. In the living room, Mr Lambchop was reading and Mrs Lambchop was mending socks.

'How nice this is, my dear,' Mr Lambchop said. 'I am enjoying my newspaper, and your company, and the thought of our boys studying in their room.'

'Let us hope they *are* studying, George,' said Mrs Lambchop. 'So often they find excuses not to work.'

Mr Lambchop chuckled. 'They are very imaginative,' he said. 'No doubt of that.'

In their bedroom, Stanley and his younger brother, Arthur, had in fact begun their homework. They wore pyjamas, and over his Arthur also wore his Mighty Man T-shirt, which helped him to concentrate.

On the desk between them was what they supposed to be a teapot – a round, rather squashed-down pot with a curving spout, and a knob on top for lifting. A wave had rolled it up onto the beach that summer, right to Stanley's feet, and since Mrs Lambchop was very fond of old furniture and silverware, he had saved it as a gift for her birthday, now only a week away.

The pot was painted dark green, but streaks of brownish metal showed through where the green had rubbed off. To see if polishing would make it shine, Stanley rubbed the knob with his pyjama sleeve.

Puff! Black smoke came from the spout.

'Yipe!' Arthur said. 'It's going to explode!'

'Teapots don't explode.' Stanley rubbed again. 'I just –'

Puff! Puff! Puff! They came rapidly now, joining to form a small cloud in the air above the desk.

'Look out!' Arthur shouted. 'Double yipes!'

The black cloud swirled within itself, and its blackness became a mixture of brown and blue. A moment more, and it began to lose its cloud shape; arms appeared, and legs, and a head.

'Ready or not, here I come!' said a clear young voice.

And then the cloud was completely gone, and a slender, cheerful-looking body hovered in the air above the desk. He wore a sort of decorated towel on his head, a loose blue shirt, and curious, flapping brown trousers, one leg of which had snagged on the pot's spout.

'Florts!' said the boy, shaking his leg. 'Collibots! I got the puffs right, and the scary cloud, but – There!' Unsnagged, he floated down to the floor and bowed to

Stanley and Arthur.

'Who rubbed?' he asked

Neither of the brothers could speak.

'Well, *someone* did. Genies don't just drop in, you know.' The boy bowed again. 'How do you do? I am Prince Fawzi Mustafa Aslan Mirza Melek Namerd Haraz. Call me Prince Haraz.'

Arthur gasped and dived under his bed.

'What's the matter with him?' the genie asked. 'And who are you, and where am I?'

'I'm Stanley Lambchop, and this is the United States of America,' Stanley said. 'That's my brother Arthur under the bed.'

'Not a very friendly welcome,' said Prince Haraz. 'Especially for someone who's been cooped up in a lamp.' Frowning, he rubbed the back of his neck. 'Florts! One thousand years, with my knees right up against my chin. This is my first time out.'

'I must have gone crazy,' said Arthur from under the bed. 'I am just going to lie here until a doctor comes.'

'Actually, Prince Haraz, you're here sort of by accident,' Stanley said. 'I didn't even know that pot was a lamp. Was it the rubbing? Those puffs of smoke, I mean, that turned into you?'

'Were you scared?' The genie laughed. 'Just a few puffs, I thought, and then I'll *whoooosh* up the spout!'

'Scaring *me* wasn't fair,' said Arthur, staying under the bed. 'I just live in this room because Stanley's my brother. It's his lamp, and he's the one who rubbed it.'

'Then he's the one I grant wishes for,' said

Prince Haraz. 'Too bad for you.'

'I don't care,' said Arthur, but he did.

'Can I wish for anything?' Stanley asked 'Anything at all?'

'Not if it's cruel or evil, or really nasty,' said Prince Haraz. 'I'm a lamp genie, you see, and we're the good kind. Not like those big jar genies. They're stinkers! Take my advice and stay away from big jars and urns – and if you do see one, don't rub it.'

'Wish for something, Stanley,' said Arthur, sounding suspicious. 'Test him out.'

'Wait,' Stanley said. 'I'll be right back.'

He went out into the living room, where Mr and Mrs Lambchop were still sitting quietly enjoying themselves.

'Hey!' he said. 'Guess what?'

'Hay is for horses, Stanley, not people,' said

Mr Lambchop from behind his newspaper. 'Try to remember that.'

'Excuse me,' Stanley said. 'But you'll never guess –'

'My guess is that you and Arthur have not yet finished your homework,' said Mrs Lambchop, looking up from her mending. 'In fact, you can hardly have begun.'

'We *were* going to do it,' said Stanley, talking very fast, 'but I have this pot that turned out to be a lamp, and when I rubbed it smoke came out and then a genie, and he says I can wish for things, only I thought maybe I should ask you first. Arthur got scared, so he's hiding under the bed.'

Mr Lambchop chuckled. 'When your studying is done, my boy,' he said. 'But no treasure chests full of gold and diamonds, please. Think of the taxes we would pay!'

'There is your answer, Stanley,' said Mrs Lambchop. 'Now back to work, please.'

'Okay, then,' said Stanley, going out.

Mrs Lambchop laughed. 'Chests full of gold and diamonds, indeed. Taxes! George, you are very amusing.'

Behind his newspaper, Mr Lambchop smiled again. 'Thank you, my dear,' he said.

The Askit Basket

'I told them, but they didn't believe me,' Stanley said, back in the bedroom.

'Of course they didn't.' Arthur was still under the bed. 'Who'd believe that a whole person could puff out of a pot?'

'It's not a *pot*,' said Prince Haraz. 'And this is a ridiculous way to carry on a conversation. Please come out. I apologize for the puffs.'

Arthur crawled from under the bed. 'No more scary stuff?'

'I promise,' the genie said, and they shook hands.

Arthur could hardly wait now. 'Try it Stanley,' he wish. 'Try a wish.'

'We're not allowed,' Stanley said. 'Not till our homework is done.'

'What's homework?' Prince Haraz asked.

The brothers stared at him, amazed, and then Stanley explained. The genie shook his head.

'*After* schooltime, when you could be having fun?' he said. 'Where I come from, we just let Askit Baskets do the work.'

'Well, whatever *they* are, I wish I had one,' said Stanley, forgetting he was not supposed to wish.

Prince Haraz laughed. 'Oh? Look behind you.'

Turning, Stanley and Arthur saw a large straw basket, about the size of a beach ball and decorated with green and red zigzag stripes, floating in the air above the desk.

'Yipes!' said Arthur. 'More scary stuff!'

'Don't be silly,' said the genie. 'It's a perfectly ordinary Askit Basket. Whatever you want to know, Stanley, just ask it.'

Feeling rather foolish, Stanley leaned forward and spoke to the basket.

'I, uh . . . that is . . . uh,' he said. 'I'd like, uh . . . can I have answers for my maths homework? It's the problems on page twenty of my book.'

The basket made a steady *huuuummm* sound, and then the hum stopped and a

man's voice rose from it, deep and rich like a TV announcer's.

'Thank you for calling Askit Baskets,' it said. 'Unfortunately, all our Answer Genies are busy at the present time, but your questions have been received, and you will be served by the first available personnel. While you wait, enjoy a selection by The Geniettes. This message will not be repeated.'

Stanley stared at the Askit Basket. Music was coming out of it now, the sort of soft, faraway music he had heard in the elevators of big office buildings.

Prince Haraz shrugged. 'What can you do? It's a very popular service.'

There was a *click* and the music stopped. Now a female voice, full of bouncy good cheer, came from the basket, 'Hi! This is Shireen. Thanks a whole bunch for waiting, and I would like at this time to give you your answers. The first answer is: 5 pears, 6 apples, 8 bananas. The second answer is: Tom is 4 years old, Tim is 7, Ted is 11. The third –'

'Let me get a pencil!' Stanley shouted. 'I can't remember all this!'

'A written record, created especially for

your own personal convenience, is in the basket, sir,' said the cheery voice. 'Thanks for calling Askit Basket, and have a nice day!'

'Wait!' Lifting the lid of the basket, Stanley saw a sheet of paper with all his answers on it. 'Oh, good!' he said. 'Thank you. Can my brother talk now, please?'

Arthur cleared his throat. 'Hello Shireen,' he said. 'This is Arthur Lambchop speaking. For English, I'm supposed to write about "What I Want to Be". Could I have it printed out, please, like Stanley's maths?'

The answer came right away. 'Certainly, Mr Lambchop. Just a teeny-tiny moment now, while we make sure the handwriting – There! All done, Mr Lambchop!'

Arthur opened the basket and found a

sheet of lined paper covered with his own handwriting. He read it aloud.

WHAT I WANT TO BE
by Arthur Lambchop.

When I grow up, I want to be President of the United States so that I can make a law not to have any more wars. And get to meet astronauts. And I would like to be handsome, only not have to go out with girls who want to get all dressed up. Most of all I would like to be the strongest man in the world, like Mighty Man, not to hurt people, but so everybody would be extra nice to me.

The End.

Arthur smiled. 'That's pretty good!' he said. 'Just what I wanted to say, Shireen.'

'I'm so glad,' said the Askit Basket. 'Bye-bye now!'

Stanley and Arthur called good-bye, and then Prince Haraz plucked the basket out of the air and set it on the desk beside his lamp.

'There! Homework's done,' he said. 'That was an awfully ordinary sort of wish, Stanley. Isn't there something special you've always wanted? Something exciting?'

Stanley knew right away what he wanted most. He had always loved animals; how exciting it would be to have his own zoo! But that would take up too much space, he thought. Just one animal then, a truly unusual pet. A lion? Yes! What fun it would be to walk down the street with a pet lion on a leash!

'I wish for a lion!' he said. 'Real, but friendly.'

'Real, but friendly,' said the gene. 'No problem.'

Stanley realized suddenly that a lion would scare people, and that an elephant would be even greater fun.

'An elephant, I mean!' he shouted. 'Not a lion. An elephant!'

'What?' said Prince Haraz. 'An eleph–? Oh, collibots! Look what you made me do!'

A most unusual head had formed in the air across the room, a head with an elephant's trunk for a nose, but with small, neat, lion-like ears. A lion's mane appeared behind the head, but then came an elephant's body and

legs in a brownish-gold lion colour, and finally a little grey elephant tail with a pretty gold ruff at the tip. All together, these parts made an animal about the size of a medium lion or a small elephant.

'My goodness!' said Stanley. 'What's that?'

'A Liophant.' Prince Haraz sounded annoyed. 'It's your fault, not mine. You overlapped your wish.'

The Liophant opened his mouth wide and went *Grrowll-HONK!* a half roar, half snort that made everyone jump. Then he sat back on his hind legs and went *pant-pant-pant* like a puppy, looking quite nice.

'Well, we got the friendly part right,' said the genie. 'The young ones mostly are.'

Stanley patted him, and Arthur tickled behind the neat little ears. The Liophant licked their hands, and Stanley was not at all sorry that he had mixed up his wish.

Just then, a knock sounded on the bedroom door, and Mrs Lambchop's voice called out, 'Homework done?'

'Come in,' Stanley said, not stopping to think, and the door opened.

'How very quiet you –' Mrs Lambchop began, and then she stopped.

Her eyes moved slowly about the room from Prince Haraz to the Askit Basket, and on to the Liophant.

'Gracious!' she said.

Prince Haraz made a little bow. 'How do you do? You are the mother of these fine lads, I suppose?'

'I am thank you,' said Mrs Lambchop. 'Have we met? I don't seem to –'

'This is Prince Haraz,' Stanley said. 'And that's a Liophant, and that's an Askit Basket.'

'Guess what,' said Arthur. 'Prince Haraz is a genie, and he'll let Stanley have anything he wants.'

'How very generous!' Mrs Lambchop said. 'But I'm not sure . . .' Turning, she called into the living room. 'George, you had better come here! Something quite unexpected has happened.'

'In a moment,' Mr Lambchop called back. 'I am reading an unusual story in my newspaper, about a duck who watches TV.'

'This is even more unusual than that,' she said, and Mr Lambchop came at once.

'Ah, yes,' he said, looking about the room. 'Yes, I see. Would someone care to explain?'

'I tried to before,' Stanley said.

'Remember? About the lamp, and –'

'Wait, dear,' said Mrs Lambchop.

The Liophant was making snuffling, hungry sounds, so she went off to the kitchen and returned with a large bowl full of hamburger mixed with warm milk. While the Liophant ate, Stanley told what had happened.

'Unusual indeed! And what a fine opportunity for you, Stanley,' Mr Lambchop said when he had heard everything, and then he frowned. 'But I do not approve of using the Askit Basket for homework, boys. Nor will your teachers, I'm afraid.'

'My plan is, let's not tell them,' Arthur said.

Mr Lambchop gave him a long look. 'Would you take credit for work you have not done?'

Arthur blushed. 'Oh, no! When you put it that way . . . Gosh, of course not! I wasn't thinking. Because of all the excitement, you know?'

Mr Lambchop wrote NOT IN USE on a piece of cardboard and taped it to the Askit Basket.

'It is too late for any more wishing tonight,' said Mrs Lambchop. 'Prince Haraz, there is a folding bed in the cupboard, so you will be quite comfortable here with Stanley and Arthur. Tomorrow is Saturday, which we Lambchops always spend together in the park. You will join us, I hope?'

'Thank you very much,' said the genie, and he helped Stanley and Arthur set up the bed.

The Liophant was already asleep, and after

Mr and Mrs Lambchop had said good night, Mrs Lambchop picked up his bowl. 'Gracious!' she said, putting out the light. 'Three pounds of the best hamburger, and he ate it all!'

It was quite dark in the bedroom, but some moonlight shone through the window. From their beds, Stanley and Arthur could see that Prince Haraz was still sitting up on his. For a moment they all kept silent, listening to the gentle snoring of the Liophant, and then the genie said, 'Sorry about that. It's having all that nose, probably.'

'It's okay,' Arthur said sleepily. 'Do genies snore?'

'We don't even sleep,' said Prince Haraz. 'Your mother was so kind, I didn't want to tell her. It might have made her feel bad.'

'I'll try to stay awake for a while, if you want to talk,' Stanley said.

'No thanks,' the genie said. 'I'll be fine. After all those years alone in the lamp, it's nice just having company.'

In the Park

Everyone slept late and enjoyed a large breakfast, particularly the Liophant, who ate two more pounds of hamburger, five bananas, and three loaves of bread.

Then, since all the Lambchops enjoyed playing tennis, they set out with their rackets for the courts in the big park close by. Since his genie clothes would make people stare, Prince Haraz borrowed slacks and a shirt from Stanley, and came along to watch.

In the street, they met Ralph Jones, an old college friend of Mr Lambchop's, whom they had not seen for quite some time.

'Nice running into you, George, and you too, Mrs Lambchop,' Mr Jones said. 'Hello, Arthur. Hello, Stanley. Aren't you the one who was flat? Rounded out nicely, I see.'

'You always did have a fine memory, Ralph,' Mr Lambchop said. 'Let me introduce our house guest, Prince Haraz. He is a foreign student, here to study our ways.'

'How do you do,' said the genie. 'I am Fawzi Mustafa Aslan Mirza Melek Namerd Haraz.'

'How do you do,' Mr Jones said. 'Well, I must be on my way. Good-bye, Lambchops. Nice to have met you, Prince Fawzi Mustafa Aslan Mirza Melek Namerd Haraz.'

'He *does* have a wonderful memory,' Mrs Lambchop said, as Mr Jones walked away.

They set out for the park again.

'Wouldn't Mr Jones be surprised if he learned Prince Haraz was a genie?' Mrs Lambchop said. 'The whole world would be amazed. Gracious! We'd all be famous, I'm sure.'

'I was famous once, when I was flat,' Stanley said. 'I didn't like it after a while.'

'I remember,' said Mrs Lambchop. 'Nevertheless, I would enjoy discovering for myself what being famous feels like.'

Prince Haraz looked at Stanley, his eyebrows raised in a questioning way. Stanley gave a little nod, and the genie smiled and nodded back.

Just ahead, near the entrance to the park, was the Famous Museum of Art, one of the most important buildings in the city. A guided-tour bus, filled with visitors from all over the United States and from many foreign countries, had stopped in front of the museum, and the driver was lecturing his passengers through a megaphone.

'Over where those trees are, that's our magnificent City Park!' shouted the driver. 'Here, on the right, is the Famous Museum of Art, with the world's most expensive paintings, statues, and – Oh, what a surprise! We're in luck today, folks! That's

Mrs George Lambchop, coming right toward us! Harriet Lambchop herself, in person! Right there, with the tennis racket!'

Cries of astonishment and pleasure rose from the tourists as they turned in their seats to stare where the driver was pointing.

'What's this?' said Mr Lambchop. 'Is that man talking about you, Harriet?'

'I think so,' said Mrs Lambchop. 'Oh, my goodness! They're coming!'

The tourists were rushing out of the bus, waving cameras and autograph pads. A Japanese family reached Mrs Lambchop first, all with cameras.

'Please, Lambchop lady,' said the husband, bowing politely. 'Honour to take picture, yes?'

'Of course,' said Mrs Lambchop. 'I hope you are enjoying our country. But why *my* picture? I'm not –'

'No, no! Famous, famous! Famous Lambchop lady!' cried the Japanese family, taking pictures as fast as they could.

Mrs Lambchop understood suddenly that her wish had been granted. 'Thank you, Stanley and Prince Haraz!' she said. 'What fun!'

She posed graciously for all the tourists and signed dozens of autographs. This took almost half an hour, and at the entrance to the park she was recognized again, and had to do more posing and signing.

It was by now mid-morning, and all the park's tennis courts were occupied, but the Lambchops' disappointment vanished quickly when they saw a crowd gathered by one court, and learned that Tom McRude, the world's best tennis player, was about to lecture and demonstrate his strokes. Tom McRude had a terrible temper and very bad manners, but because of his wonderful tennis a great many people had come to see him. The Lambchops and Prince Haraz managed to squeeze close to the court, next to the television news cameras that were covering the event.

'None of you can ever be a great tennis player like me,' Tom McRude was saying, out on the court. 'But at least you can have the thrill of getting to see me.'

A little old lady in the crowd gave a tiny sneeze, and he glared at her. 'What's the matter with you, granny?' he shouted.

The old lady burst into tears, and her friends led her away.

'What a mean fellow!' Prince Haraz whispered in Stanley.

'I can't stand old sneezing people!' said Tom McRude. 'Okay, now I'm going to show how I hit my great forehand! First, I —'

'Hold it, Tom!' called the television director. 'We've just spotted Harriet Lambchop in the crowd here. What a break! Maybe we can get her to say a few words to our audience!'

Even Tom McRude was impressed. '*The* Harriet Lambchop? Here? In person?'

'Swing those cameras this way, fellows!' The director ran to where the Lambchops were standing, and held a microphone out to Mrs Lambchop.

'Wonderful to see you!' he said. 'Everybody wants to know what you think. What about the foreign situation? What's your favourite colour? Go to discos? Do you sleep in pyjamas or a nightdress?'

'Isn't that rather personal?' said Mr Lambchop.

'George, please. . . .' Mrs Lambchop smiled at the director. 'Thank you for your kind welcome,' she said into the microphone, 'and I would just like to say at this time that I hope all my fans are having a lovely day here in this delightful park.'

The crowd cheered and waved, and Mrs Lambchop waved back and blew a few kisses. Tom McRude was so jealous of the attention she was getting that he whacked a tennis ball angrily over the trees behind the court. Noticing, Mrs Lambchop spoke again into the microphone.

'And now,' she said, 'do let us hear what this champion athlete has to tell us about tennis.'

'Yeah!' growled Tom McRude at the TV man. 'Get those cameras back on me!'

When the cameras had swung back to him again, he said, 'Now I want a volunteer, so that I can demonstrate how terrible most players are compared to me.'

Mr Lambchop thought how exciting it would be to venture onto the same court with the champion. Signalling with his racket, he stepped forward.

'Okay.' Tom McRude handed over some balls. 'Let's see how you serve.'

Mr Lambchop prepared to serve.

'He's got his feet wrong!' Tom McRude shouted to the crowd. 'And his grip is wrong! Everything is wrong!'

This made Mr Lambchop so nervous that he served two balls into the net instead of over it.

'Terrible, terrible! Watch how I do it,' said Tom McRude, running to the far side of the court. From there, he served five balls in a row to Mr Lambchop, so hard and fast that Mr Lambchop missed the first four entirely. The fifth one knocked the racket out of his hand.

'Ha, ha!' laughed Tom McRude. 'Now let's see you run!'

He began hitting whizzing forehands and backhands at sharp angles across the court, making Mr Lambchop look very foolish indeed as he raced back and forth, getting redder and redder in the face and missing practically every shot.

The other Lambchops grew very angry as they watched, and Prince Haraz saw how they felt. 'This need not continue, you know,' he whispered to Stanley.

Just then, Mr Lambchop came skidding to a halt before them, banging his knee with his racket as he missed another of the champion's powerful shots.

'Ha, ha! This is how *I* give lessons!' shouted Tom McRude.

Mr Lambchop's eyes met Stanley's, and then he looked at Prince Haraz.

'Okay,' Stanley said, and Prince Haraz smiled his little smile again.

'Thank you,' said Mr Lambchop. Returning to the court, he addressed the crowd. 'Ladies and gentlemen!' he said. 'I will try my serve again!'

Across the net, Tom McRude laughed a nasty laugh and slashed his big racket through the air.

Mr Lambchop served a ball, not into the net this time, but right where it was supposed to go, as fast as a bullet. Tom McRude could only blink as it went past him. Then his mouth fell open. 'Out!' he shouted. 'That ball was out!'

Voices rose from the crowd. 'Shame on you! . . . It was *in*! . . . What a liar! . . . In, in in!'

Tom McRude shook his fist at Mr Lambchop. 'I'll bet you can't do that again!'

Mr Lambchop served three more times, each serve even faster than the first one, and as perfectly placed. Tom McRude could not even touch them, except for the last, which bounced up into his nose.

Then Mr Lambchop began to rally with
him, gliding swiftly about the court and
returning every shot with ease. With
powerful forehands and backhands, he
made Tom McRude run from corner to
corner; with little drop shots, he drew the
champion up to the net, then lobbed

marvellous high shots that sent him racing back again. Nobody has ever played such great tennis as Mr Lambchop played that day.

Tom McRude was soon too exhausted, and too angry, to continue. He threw down his racket and jumped on it, and hurled the broken pieces into the net.

'You're just lucky!' he yelled. 'Besides, I have a cold. And the sun was in my eyes the whole time!' He pushed his way through the crowd and ran out of the park.

There was tremendous clapping and cheering for Mr Lambchop, who just smiled modestly and waved his racket in a friendly way. Then he came over to where Stanley and Arthur and Mrs Lambchop and Prince Haraz were standing with the television director.

'You're really *good*,' the director said. 'Frankly, you looked terrible when you first went there.'

'It takes me a while to get warmed up,' Mr Lambchop said, and led his family away.

In the excitement of the tennis, they had all forgotten Mrs Lambchop's fame, but on the way home she was asked again and again for her autograph, and when they arrived, a photographer and reporter from *Famous Faces* magazine were waiting.

'We want you on the cover of our next issue,' said the photographer.

'I'm supposed to do an interview,' said the reporter. 'Who do you think is sexy? How much do you weigh? Eat health foods? Will there be a movie about your life? Who gave you your first kiss?'

'None of your business!' said Mr Lambchop, and Mrs Lambchop told the *Famous Faces* people to go away.

They all watched the evening news on television, hoping Mr Lambchop's amazing tennis would be shown, but only Mrs Lambchop appeared, with Tom McRude in the background. 'The celebrated Harriet Lambchop was in the park today,' said the newscaster, after which there was a close-up of Mrs Lambchop saying, 'I hope all my fans are having a lovely day,' and that was that.

Mr Lambchop said he didn't care, but he did mind that dinner was interrupted several times by phone calls for Mrs Lambchop from newspaper and magazine and television people. The interruptions didn't both the Liophant, who ate four pork chops, a jar of peanut butter, a quart of potato salad, and the rubber mat from under his dish.

Chapter Four

The Brothers Fly

'I'm not complaining,' said Arthur, complaining, 'but it's not fair. Some people get to have Liophants and be famous. I want to be President, or as strong as Mighty Man, but all I got was one minute with an Askit Basket I'm not even allowed to use any more.'

He was talking to Stanley and Prince Haraz. It was after dinner, and they were in their bedroom, all in slippers and pyjamas.

'It's not my fault.' Prince Haraz looked hurt. 'A genie just follows orders. Rub, I appear. Wish, I grant. That's it.'

Stanley felt a little sorry for his brother. 'I don't think you ought to be President, Arthur,' he said. 'But I'll wish for you to be the strongest man in the world.' He nodded to Prince Haraz. 'Right now.'

'Oh, good!' Arthur said.

He waited, but nothing happened.

'Darn!' he said, 'I knew it wouldn't work!' Disappointed, he punched his left hand with his right fist.

'Owwww!' Jumping up and down, he waved his hand to relieve the pain.

'When you're the strongest man in the world,' Prince Haraz said, 'you have to be careful what you hit.'

'But I still feel like me,' Arthur said. Testing himself, he took hold of the big desk with one hand and lifted. It rose easily into the air above his head.

Stanley's mouth flew open, and so did the desk drawers. Pencils, paper clips, marbles, and other odds and ends rained down onto the floor.

'Oooops,' Arthur said, and lowered the desk.

'This is ridiculous,' said Prince Haraz,

helping him to tidy up. 'The strongest man in the world, in his bedroom picking up desks! Out having adventures, that's where you ought to be.'

'We can't have adventures now,' Arthur said. 'It's almost bedtime.'

Stanley had an idea. 'There'd be time if we could fly! Why can't we all fly somewhere?'

'I've always been able,' said Prince Haraz. 'For you two, it'll take wishing.'

'I wish!' Stanley shouted. 'Flying! Arthur and me both!'

Full of excitement, the brothers held their breath, thinking they would be swept up into the air, but they weren't. After a moment, Arthur tried a few small flapping movements with is elbows.

'Oh, collibots!' said the genie. 'Not like that. Just *think* of flying, and where you want to go.'

It worked.

Stanley and Arthur found themselves suddenly a few feet off the floor, face down and quite comfortable, and however they wished to go, up or down, forward or back, was the way then went. It was like swimming in soft, invisible water, but without the effort of swimming. After only a few minutes of practice, the brothers were gliding happily about the bedroom, with Prince Haraz giving advice: 'Point your toes, that helps . . . Heads up . . . Good, very good. Yes, I think you're ready now.'

He opened the window and leaned out. 'Nice enough,' he said. 'But there may be

coolish winds higher up. We'd better wear something extra.'

Stanley and Arthur put on dressing-gowns and gloves, and the genie borrowed a red parka and a woollen dragon-face ski mask.

'Away we go!' he said, and the brothers floated through the window after him, out into the night.

Up! Up! Up! UP! they went, levelling off now and then to practise speeding, but mostly rising steadily higher. Stanley and Arthur flew side by side, gaining confidence from each other, and the genie kept an eye on them from behind.

It was a beautiful night. The sky above them was full of stars, and the lights of the city, far below, twinkled as brightly as the stars. The brothers' white dressing-gowns shone in the moonlight, and the genie's parka was a glowing red.

They flew above the big park, where an orchestra was giving a concert. Music floated up to them: the clear, sweet tones of flutes and violins and trumpets; the deep, strong notes of cymbals and drums.

'Oh, I'm enjoying this!' Prince Haraz called through his dragon mask. 'So different from inside that lamp!'

They joined hands and circled together, swooping and swaying in time to the music, going round and round above the blaze of light from where the orchestra sat. It was like ice-skating to music at a rink, but much more fun.

In the distance, the blinking wing lights of a big aeroplane moved steadily across the sky.

'Let's chase it!' Stanley shouted.

'Go on! I'll catch up!' Prince Haraz laughed and let them go.

Whoooosh! *Whoooosh*! With their arms by their sides, Stanley and Arthur flashed like rockets across the sky. Their dressing-gowns made little flapping sounds, like the sails of a boat racing before the wind.

The big aeroplane was fast, but the brothers were much faster. When they caught up, they were able to fly all around the plane, looking through the windows at the passengers reading and eating from tiny trays.

Arthur saw a little girl reading a comic magazine. Zooming in close to her window, he stretched his neck, trying to read over her shoulder. The little girl looked up and saw him. Being mean, she held the magazine down between her knees where he couldn't see it, and then she stuck out her tongue. Arthur stuck his tongue out at her, and the little girl scowled and pulled the curtain across her window.

On the other side of the plane. Stanley saw a young couple with a crying baby across their laps. They looked very tired, but they were being kept awake. Stanley flew up next to the window so that the baby could see him over its parents' shoulders, and then he made a funny face, puffing out his lips and wrinkling his nose. The baby smiled, and Stanley put his thumbs in his ears and wriggled his other fingers. The baby smiled again, and closed its eyes and went to sleep.

Stanley flew around the plane, past the

cockpit, to join Arthur on the other side.

There were two pilots in the cockpit, and one of them saw Stanley fly by. Turning his head slowly, he saw both brothers hovering above a wing tip, waiting for Prince Haraz to catch up.

'Guess what I see out there, Bert,' he said.

'The stars in the sky, Max, and below us the mighty ocean,' answered the other pilot.

'No,' said Max. 'Two kids in dressing-gowns.'

'Ha, ha! You are some joker!' said Bert, but he turned to look.

Only Prince Haraz could be seen now above the wing, his parka flapping as he looked around for Stanley and Arthur, who were hiding from him behind the plane.

'So what do you see, Bert?' asked Max, keeping his own eyes straight ahead. 'Two kids in dressings-gowns, right?'

'Wrong,' said Bert quietly. 'I see a guy in ski clothes with a dragon face.'

The two pilots stared at each other, and then looked out at the wing again, but the genie had flown to join the boys behind the plane.

'Nobody there,' said Max. 'Let's never mention this to anyone, Bert. Okay?'

'Good idea,' Bert answered. 'Definitely.'

They made plane go faster and had nothing more to say.

A giant ocean liner, ablaze with lights, made its way across the sea below.

'Come on!' Arthur shouted. He whizzed away, Stanley behind him, and again Prince Haraz laughed and let them go.

The size and beauty of the great ship made

the brothers cry out in wonder as they drew near. It was like an enormous birthday cake, each deck a layer sparkling with the brightness of a thousand candles.

'Look, Stanley!' Arthur pointed. 'They're having a big party on the main deck!'

They flew closer to enjoy the fun, and then they saw that it was not a party, but a robbery.

The main deck was crowded because masked robbers had lined up all the passengers, and were taking their money and jewellery and watches. The helicopter in which the robbers had landed was parked just below the captain's bridge, which overlooked the main deck. The captain and the other ship's officers had been chained up on the bridge. They had struggled, but now

there was nothing they could do.

'We've got to help, Stanley!' Arthur said.

He zoomed down to the bridge, and shouted over the railing at the robbers on the deck below. 'Stop, you crooks! Give back all that money and jewellery and other stuff!'

Using his great strength, Arthur tore away the ropes and chains that bound the ship's officers. It was as easy for him as if he were tearing up paper.

The robbers were amazed. Unable to believe their eyes, they stumbled back from their victims, dropping money and jewellery all over the deck.

'Oh, lordy!' one robber yelled. 'Who are you?'

Remembering his favourite comic-magazine hero, Arthur could not resist showing off. He flew ten feet up in the air and stayed there, looking fierce.

'I am Mighty Arthur!' he shouted in a deep voice. 'Mighty Arthur, Enemy of Crime!'

Exclamations rose from the robbers and passengers and ship's officers. 'So strong, and a flier too! . . . Who expected Mighty Arthur? . . . Are we ever lucky! . . . This ought to be on TV!'

Now Stanley came swooping down from the sky with his dressing-gown belt untied, so that the gown flared behind him like a cape.

'And I'm Mighty Stanley!' he called. 'Defender of the Innocent!'

'I do that too!' cried Arthur, wishing he had made his robe a cape. 'We both do good things, but I'm the really strong one!'

Several robbers were trying to escape in the helicopter, and he saw another chance to prove his strength.

The helicopter was already rising, but Arthur flashed through the air until he was directly above it, and with one hand he pushed it back onto the deck. When the frightened robbers jumped out, the ship's officers grabbed them and tied them up.

Now the passengers were even more excited and amazed. 'Did you see that?' they said, and 'Mighty Arthur and Mighty Stanley, both on the same day!' and 'This is *better* than TV!'

The brothers flew up to join Prince Haraz, who had been circling over the ship. 'What a pair of show-offs!' said the genie, as they set out for home. 'Even worse than I used to be.'

Behind them, cheers floated up from the grateful passengers and crew. 'Hooray for our rescuers!' they heard, and 'Especially Mighty Arthur!' which was followed a moment later by 'Mighty Stanley too, of course!'

Soon the big ship was no more than an outline of tiny lights in the black sea below, and the last cheer was only a whisper above the rushing of the wind. 'Three cheers . . . for . . . the Enemy . . . of . . . Crime . . . and the . . . Defender . . . of the Inno . . . cent!'

The brothers felt very proud, but it had been a tiring adventure, and they were not sorry when the city came into sight.

Chapter Five

The Last Wish

When the three adventurers flew just into the bedroom, the Liophant was just finishing an enormous bowl of spaghetti mixed with chocolate cookies and milk. He looked sleepy, but Mr and Mrs Lambchop, standing by the door, were very much awake.

'Thank goodness you are all right!' Mrs Lambchop ran to hug her sons.

Mr Lambchop's voice was stern. 'Where

have you been? Is that you, Prince Haraz, behind the dragon face?'

The genie took off his ski mask. 'Were you worried?' he said. 'Sorry. We just went for a little flight.'

'Wait till you hear!' said Arthur. 'You can't tell from looking, but I'm the strongest man in the world, and –'

'First take off those dressings-gowns and gloves,' said Mrs Lambchop. 'It is not wise to get overheated.'

She went on talking while they put their things away. 'What a *dreadful* evening! The phone never stopped ringing. I was asked to go on six television shows, and to be in an advertisement for a new kind of soap – they wanted pictures of me in the bathtub, so of course I said no! – and to sit with the mayor during the next parade. I'm exhausted! And such a fright, after all that, to find the window open and the three of you gone!'

'We thought we'd be right back,' said Stanley, apologising. 'We didn't know so many exciting things would happen.'

Everyone sat down, and he explained about wishing Arthur strong, and the flying not leaving out how they had chased the aeroplane and startled the robbers on the great ship at sea. Mr and Mrs Lambchop looked more and more worried as they listened, and when Stanley was done, Mr Lambchop gave a deep sigh.

'It seems, Prince Haraz,' he said, 'that there are often unexpected consequences when wishes come true.'

The genie nodded. 'I'll say. That's how I got

myself put into a lamp.'

'It is not just the difficulty about the Askit Basket,' Mr Lambchop said. 'Mrs Lambchop has been famous for only a day, and already it has exhausted her and cost our family its privacy. And though Tom McRude deserved the lessons he got, his tennis comes from natural ability, and I am not proud of having shamed him by the use of magic.'

'And now Arthur is so strong that other boys will be afraid to play with him,' said Mrs Lambchop. 'And this flying, and getting mixed up with criminals – Oh, it *is* worrying!'

'Indeed it is,' Mr Lambchop said. 'We must all think hard about what has happened, and what the future may bring.'

'I will make hot chocolate,' said Mrs

Lambchop. 'It is extremely helpful when there is serious thinking to be done.'

Everyone enjoyed the delicious hot chocolate she brought from the kitchen, with a marshmallow for each cup. Mr and Mrs Lambchop and Stanley and Arthur sat with their eyes half closed, sipping and thinking. Prince Haraz kept silent for a while, and then he said he was sorry to have cause problems, and began to pace up and down. The Liophant went to sleep.

At last Mr Lambchop put down his cup and cleared his throat. 'May I have your attention, please?' he said.

When they were all looking at him, he said. 'Here is my opinion. Genies and their magic, Prince Haraz, may be well suited to faraway lands and long-ago times, but the

Lambchops have always been quite ordinary people, and this is the United States of America, and the time is today. We are grateful, I'm sure, for the excitement you have brought us, but I now believe that it would have been better for everyone if you had remained in your lamp. And so I must ask: Is is possible for Stanley to unwish the wishes he has made?'

'There is a way, actually,' said Prince Haraz, looking surprised.

Mrs Lambchop clapped her hands. 'How very wise you are, George! Don't you agree, boys?'

Arthur wasn't sure. 'I really like the flying,' he said, and then he sighed. 'But being so strong . . . I guess nobody *would* play with me.'

'What I care most about is the Liophant,' Stanley said. 'Couldn't we just keep him?'

'He *is* very lovable,' Mrs Lambchop said. 'But he *eats* so much! We cannot afford to keep him.'

'Sad, my dear, but true,' said Mr Lambchop. 'Now tell us, Prince Haraz, how we are

to proceed.'

'It's called Reverse Wishing,' said the genie.

The little green lamp was still on the desk,
and he picked it up and turned it over. 'The
instructions should be right here,' he said.
'Let's see. . . .'

The Lambchops waited anxiously as he

studied the words that had been carved into the bottom of the lamp.

'Simple enough,' he said, after a moment. 'Each wish has to be reversed separately. I just say "Mandrono!" and –' His voice rose. 'Oh, collibots! Double florts! See that little circle there? This is a training lamp! There may not be enough wishes left!'

'What?' exclaimed Mr Lambchop. 'What's a training lamp?'

'They're used for beginners like me, so we don't do too much for one person,' Prince Haraz said unhappily. 'The number in the circle, the fifteen, that's all the wishes I'm allowed to grant Stanley.'

The Lambchops all spoke at once. 'What? . . . Only fifteen? . . . You never said! . . . Oh dear!'

'Please, I'm embarrassed enough,' said the

genie, very red in the face. 'A training lamp! As if I were a baby!'

'We are all beginners at one time or another,' Mr Lambchop said. 'What matters now is, are fifteen wishes enough?'

Prince Haraz counted, folding his fingers to be sure he got it right. 'Askit Basket, Liophant – lucky he doesn't count double – that's two, and fame for Mrs Lambchop and the fancy tennis, that's four. Making Arthur strong, five, and flying for him *and* Stanley is two more . . .' He smiled. 'Seven, and seven for the reversing is fourteen! And we have a wish left over for some sort of good-bye treat!'

'Thank goodness!' said Mrs Lambchop. 'Could you manage all the reversing right now, please? It has grown very late.'

'I'll do the whole family in a bunch,' said the genie. 'Let's see. . . . Strength, famous, tennis, two flying. Ready, Arthur? No more Mighty Man after this, I'm afraid.'

'Will I feel weak?' Arthur asked. 'Will I flop over?'

The genie shook his head. 'Mandrono!' he said. 'Mandrono, Mandrono, Mandrono, Mandrono!'

Arthur felt a curious but not unpleasant prickling on the back of his neck. When the prickling stopped, he gave the big desk a shove, but it didn't move.

'I'm just the regular me again,' he said. 'Oh, well.'

'And I am just Harriet Lambchop again,' said Mrs Lambchop, smiling. 'An unimportant person.'

'To all of us, my dear, you are the most important person we know,' Mr Lambchop said. 'Arthur, you are as strong as you were yesterday. Think of it that way.'

Prince Haraz sipped the last of his hot chocolate. 'Where was I? Oh, yes . . .' He glanced at the Askit Basket, said, 'Mandrono!' and the basket was gone. 'That leaves just the Liophant,' he said.

The Lambchops all turned to look at the Liophant who was awake now and sitting up in the corner, trying to scratch behind his lion ears with the tip of his elephant trunk. Stanley went over and patted him, and the Liophant licked his hand.

'How sweet!' said Mrs Lambchop. 'George, perhaps . . .?'

'What makes Liophants happiest,' the genie

said, 'is open spaces, and chasing unicorns, and wrestling with other Liophants.'

'Then send him where it's like that,' said

Stanley, patting again. The Liophant vanished halfway through the pat.

For a moment no one spoke. Then Mr Lambchop put his hand on Stanley's shoulder in a sympathetic way. 'Good for you,' he said.

Stanley sat down to think about the one wish he had left, and Mrs Lambchop began to collect the hot-chocolate cups. 'Where will you go, Prince Haraz, when you leave us?' she asked.

'Right back into that stuffy little lamp,' said the genie. 'And then it's just wait, wait, wait! Another thousand years, at least. It's a punishment I got for playing too many tricks. My friends warned me, but I wouldn't listen.'

Sighing, he handed Mrs Lambchop his

empty cup. 'Mosef, Ali, Ben Sifa, little Fawz. Such wonderful fellows! I think of them when I'm alone in the lamp, the fun they must be having, the games, the freedom . . .'

The genie's voice trembled, and he turned his head away. All the Lambchops felt very sorry for him.

Then Arthur had an idea. He ran across the room to whisper it to Stanley.

'Whispering?' said Mrs Lambchop. 'Where are your manners, dear?'

'Who cares?' Prince Haraz said crossly. 'Let's have that last wish, and I'll smoke back into my lamp.'

The brothers were smiling at each other.

'Good idea, right?' said Arthur.

'Oh, yes!' Stanley said.

He turned to the genie. 'Here is my last

wish, Prince Haraz. I wish for you not to stay in the lamp, but to go back where you came from, so that you can be with your genie friends and have good times with them, forever from now on!'

Prince Haraz gasped. His mouth fell open.

Mr Lambchop worried that he might faint. 'Are you all right?' he asked. 'Is Stanley not allowed to set you free?'

'Oh, yes. . . .' The genie's voice was very low. 'It's allowed. But whoever heard of . . . That is, nobody ever used up a wish for the sake of a genie. Not until now.'

'How very selfish people can be!' said Mrs Lambchop.

Prince Haraz rubbed his eyes. 'What a fine family this is!' he said, beginning to smile. 'I thank you all. The name of Lambchop will be honoured always, wherever genies meet.'

His smile enormous now, he shook hands with each of the Lambchops. The last shake was with Stanley, and the genie was already a bit smoky about the edges. By the time he let go of Stanley's hand, he was all smoke, a dark cloud that swirled briefly over the little lamp on the desk, and then poured in through the spout until not a puff remained.

Full of wonder, the Lambchops gathered about the lamp, and after a moment Arthur put his lips to the spout.

'Good-bye, Prince Haraz!' he called. 'have a nice trip!'

From inside the lamp, faint and far away, a voice cried, 'Bless you, bless you all . . .' and then there was only silence in the room.

'I am proud of you, Stanley,' Mr Lambchop

said. 'Your last wish was generous and kind.'

'It was my idea, actually,' Arthur said, and Mrs Lambchop kissed the top of his head.

Then she gathered the last of the hot-chocolate cups and put them on her tray. 'Off to bed now,' she said. 'Tomorrow is another day.'

Stanley and Arthur got into bed, and she turned out the light.

'The lamp was supposed to be a surprise birthday present,' Stanley said sleepily. 'Now it won't be a surprise anymore.'

'I will love my present when you give it to me,' said Mrs Lambchop. 'And Prince Haraz was a tremendous surprise. Good night, boys.'

She kissed them both, and so did Mr Lambchop, and they went out.

The brothers lay quietly in the darkness for

a while, and then Stanley sighed. 'I miss the Liophant a little,' he said. 'But I don't mind about the rest.'

'Me neither,' Arthur yawned. 'Florts, Stanley, and good night.'

'Good night,' Stanley said. 'Collibots.'

'Mandrono,' murmured Arthur, and soon they were both asleep.

by Jeff Brown
Pictures by Scott Nash

EGMONT

CONTENTS

Prologue

She was the sort of little girl who liked to be *sure* of things, so she went all over Snow City, checking up.

The elves had done their work.

At the Post Office, Mail Elves had read the letters, making lists of who wanted what.

In the great workshops – the Doll Room, the Toy Plant, the Game Mill –

Gift Elves had filled the orders, taking care as to colour and size and style.

In the Wrap Shed the gifts lay ready, wrapped now in gay paper with holly and pine cones, sorted by country, by city or village, by road or lane or street.

The Wrap Elves teased her. 'Don't trust us, eh? . . . Snooping, we call this, Miss!'

'Pooh!' said the little girl. 'Well done, elves! Good work!'

But at home in Snow City Square, all was not well.

'Don't slam the door, dear,' said her mother weeping. 'Your father's having his nap.'

'Mother! What's wrong?'

'He won't go this year, he says!' the mother sobbed. 'He's been so cross lately, but I never –'

'*Why*? *Why* won't he go?'

'They've lost faith, don't care any more, he says! Surely not *everyone*, I said. Think of your favourite letter, the one by your desk! He just growled at me!'

'Pooh!' said the girl. 'It's not fair! Really! I mean, everything's *ready*! Why –'

'Not now, dear,' said the mother. 'It's been a dreadful day.'

In the little office at the back of the house, the girl studied the letter her mother had mentioned, framed with others on a wall:

I am a regular boy, except that I got flat, the letter said. *From an accident. I was going to ask for new clothes, but my mother already bought them. She had to, because of the flatness. So I'm just writing to say don't*

bother about me. Have a nice holiday. My
father says be careful driving, there are lots
of bad drivers this time of year.

The girl thought for a moment, and an idea came to her. 'Hmmmm . . . Well, why *not*?' she said.

She looked again at the letter.

The name LAMBCHOP was printed across the top, and an address. It was signed 'Stanley, USA.'

Chapter One

Sarah

It was two nights before Christmas, and all through the house not a Lambchop was stirring, but something was.

Stanley Lambchop sat up in his bed. 'Listen! Someone said "Rat."'

'It was more like "grat,"' said his younger brother Arthur, from his bed. 'In the living room, I think.'

The brothers tiptoed down the stairs.

For a moment all was silence in the darkened living room. Then came a *thump*. 'Ouch!' said a small voice. 'Drat again!'

'Are you a burglar?' Arthur called. 'Did you hurt yourself?'

'I am *not* a burglar!' said the voice. 'Where's the – ah!' The lights came on.

The brothers stared.

Before the fireplace, by the Christmas tree, stood a slender, dark-haired little girl wearing a red jacket and skirt, both trimmed with white fur.

'I banged it *twice*,' she said, rubbing her knee. 'Coming down the chimney, and just now.'

'We *do* have a front door, you know,' said Stanley.

'Well, so does my house. But, you know, this time of year . . .?' The girl sounded a

bit nervous. 'Actually, I've never done this before. Let's see . . . Ha, ha, ha! Season's Greetings! Ha, ha, ha!'

'"Ha, ha!" to you,' said Arthur. 'What's so funny?'

'Funny?' said the girl. 'Oh! "Ho, ho, ho!" I meant. I'm Sarah Christmas. Who are you?'

'Arthur Lambchop,' said Arthur. 'That's my brother Stanley.'

'It is? But he's not *flat*.'

'He was, but I blew him up,' Arthur explained. 'With a bicycle pump.'

'Oh, no! I wish you hadn't.' Sarah Christmas sank into a chair. 'Drat! It's all going wrong! Perhaps I shouldn't have come. But that's how I am. Headstrong, my mother says. She –'

'Excuse me,' Stanley said. 'But where are

you from?'

'And why *did* you come?' said Arthur.

Sarah told them.

Mr and Mrs Lambchop were reading in bed.

A tap came at the door, and then Stanley's voice. 'Hey! Can I come in?'

Mr and Mrs Lambchop cared greatly for

proper speech. 'Hay is for horses, Stanley,' she said. 'And not "can" dear. You *may* come in.'

Stanley came in.

'What is the explanation, my boy, of this late call?' said Mr Lambchop, remembering past surprises. 'You have not, I see, become flat again. Has a genie come to visit? Or perhaps the President of the United States has called?'

Mrs Lambchop smiled. 'You are very amusing, George.'

'Arthur and I were in bed,' said Stanley. 'But we heard a noise and went to see. It was a girl called Sarah Christmas, from Snow City. She talks a lot. She says her father says he won't come this year, but Sarah thinks he might change his mind if I ask him to. Because I wrote him a letter once that he liked. She wants me to go with her to Snow City. In her father's sleigh. It's at the North Pole, I think.' Stanley caught his breath. 'I said I'd have to ask you first.'

'Quite right,' said Mrs Lambchop.

Mr Lambchop went to the bathroom and drank a glass of water to calm himself.

'Now then, Stanley,' he said, returning. 'You have greatly startled us. Surely –'

'Put on your robe, George,' said Mrs Lambchop. 'Let us hear for ourselves what this visitor has to say.'

'This is *delicious*!' Sarah Christmas sipped the hot chocolate Mrs Lambchop had served them all. 'My mother makes it too, with cinnamon in it. And little cookies with –' Her glance had fallen on the

mantelpiece. 'What's *that*, pinned up there?'

'Christmas stockings,' Stanley said. 'The blue one's mine.'

'But the other, the great square thing?'

'It's a pillow case.' Arthur blushed. 'My stocking wouldn't do. I have very small feet.'

'Pooh!' Sarah laughed. 'You wanted extra gifts, so –'

'Sarah, dear,' Mrs Lambchop said. 'Your father? Has he truly made up his mind, you think?'

'Oh, yes!' Sarah sighed. 'But I thought – Stanley being flat, that *really* interested him. I mean, I couldn't be *sure*, but if nobody ever did anything without –'

'You seem a very nice girl, Sarah.' Mr Lambchop gave a little laugh. 'But you *have* been joking with us, surely? I –'

The phone rang, and he answered it.

'Hello, George,' the caller said. 'This is your neighbour, Frank Smith. I know it's late, but I must congratulate you on your

Christmas lawn display! Best –'

'Lawn?' said Mr Lambchop. 'Display?'

'The sleigh! And those life-like *reindeer*! What makes them move about like that? Batteries, I suppose?'

'Just a moment, Frank.' Mr Lambchop went to the window and looked out, Mrs Lambchop beside him.

'My goodness!' she said. 'One, two, three, four . . . eight! And such a pretty sleigh!'

Mr Lambchop returned to the phone. 'They *are* life-like, aren't they? Goodbye. Thank you for calling, Frank.'

'See? I'm not a joking kind of person, actually,' said Sarah Christmas. 'Now! My idea *might* work, even without the flatness. Do let Stanley go!'

'To the North Pole?' said Mrs Lambchop. 'At night? By himself? Good

gracious, Sarah!'

'It's not fair, asking Stanley, but not me,' said Arthur, feeling hurt. 'It's always like this! I never –'

'Oh, pooh!' Sarah Christmas smiled. 'Actually . . . You could *all* go. It's a very big sleigh.'

Mr and Mrs Lambchop looked at each other, then at Stanley and Arthur, then at each other again.

'Stanley just might make a difference, George,' Mrs Lambchop said. 'And if we can *all* go . . . ?'

'Quite right,' said Mr Lambchop. 'Sarah, we will accompany you to Snow City!'

'Hooray!' shouted Stanley and Arthur, and Sarah too.

Mrs Lambchop thought they should wait until Frank Smith had gone to bed.

'Imagine the gossip,' she said, 'were he to see our reindeer fly away.'

Mr Lambchop called his office to leave a message on the night-time answering machine. He would not be in tomorrow, he said, as he had been called unexpectedly out of town.

'There!' cried Stanley, by the window. 'The Smiths' light is out.'

The Lambchops changed quickly from pyjamas to warmer clothing, and followed Sarah to the sleigh.

Chapter Two

The Sleigh

'Welcome aboard!' said Sarah, from the driver's seat.

The Lambchops, sitting on little benches that made the big sleigh resemble a roofless bus, could scarcely contain their excitement.

The night sky shone bright with stars, and from the windows of nearby houses red and green Christmas lights twinkled over snowy lawns and streets. Before them, the eight reindeer, fur shiny in the moonlight, tossed their antlered heads.

'Ready when you are, Sarah,' Mr Lambchop said.

'Good!' Sarah cleared her throat. 'Fasten your seat belts, please! We are about to depart for Snow City. My name is Sarah – I guess you know that – and I'll be glad to answer any questions you may have. Please do not move about without permission of the Sleigh Master – that's me, at least right now – and obey whatever instructions may –'

'Puleeese!' said Arthur.

'Oh, all right!' The Lambchops fastened their seat belts, and Sarah took up the reins. 'Ready, One? Ready, Two, Three –'

'Just *numbers*?' cried Mrs Lambchop.

'Why, we know such lovely reindeer names! Dasher, Dancer, Prancer, Vixen –'

'Comet, Cupid, Donder, Blitzen!' shouted Arthur. 'They're from a poem we know!'

'Those *are* good names!' said Sarah. 'Ready, One through Eight?'

The reindeer pawed the ground, jingling their harness bells.

'Now!' said Sarah.

The jingling stopped suddenly, and a great silence fell.

Now a silver mist rose, swirling, about the sleigh. The startled Lambchops could see nothing beyond the mist, not their house nor the houses of their neighbours, not the twinkling Christmas lights, not the bright stars above. There was only the silver mist, everywhere, cool

against their cheeks.

'What is this, Sarah?' Mrs Lambchop called. 'Are we not to proceed to Snow City?'

Sarah's voice came cheerfully through the mist. 'We have proceeded. We're there!'

Chapter Three

Snow City

Beyond the mist, excited voices rose. 'Sarah's back! . . . With strangers! Big ones! . . . Where's she been?'

'Poppa's elves,' said Sarah's voice. As she spoke, the mist swirled, then vanished as suddenly as it had come. Above them, the stars shone bright again.

The sleigh rested now in a snow-covered square, in front of a pretty red-roofed

house. All about the square were tiny cottages, their windows aglow with light.

Elves surrounded the sleigh. 'Who *are* these people? . . . Is it true, what we've heard? . . . Ask Sarah! She'll know!'

The Lambchops smiled and waved. The elves seemed much like ordinary men and women, except that they had pointy ears, very wrinkled faces, and were only about half as tall as Arthur. All wore leather breeches or skirts with wide pockets from which tools and needles stuck out.

'Miss Sarah!' came a voice. 'Is it true? He won't go this year?'

Sarah hesitated. 'Well, sort of . . . But perhaps the Lambchops here . . . Be patient. Go home, please!'

The elves straggled off toward their cottages, grumbling. 'Not going? . . . Hah! After all our work? . . . The *Who*chops? . . . I'd go work somewhere else, but *where*?'

A plump lady in an apron bustled out of the red-roofed house. 'Sarah! Are you all right? Going off like that! Though we did find your note. Gracious! Are those *all* Lambchops, dear?'

'I'm fine, Momma!' said Sarah. 'They wouldn't let Stanley come by himself. That's Stanley, there. The other one's Arthur. Stanley *was* flat, but he got round again.'

'Clever!' said Mrs Christmas. 'Well! Do all come in! Are you fond of hot chocolate?'

'. . . an excellent plan, I do see that. But – Oh, he's in *such* a state! And with Stanley no longer flat . . .' Mrs Christmas sighed. 'More chocolate, Lambchops? I add a dash of cinnamon. Tasty, yes?'

'Delicious,' said Mrs Lambchop.

Everyone sat silent, sipping.

Mr Lambchop felt the time had come. 'May we see him now, Mrs Christmas? We should be getting home. So much to do, this time of year.'

'You forget where you are, George,' said Mrs Lambchop. 'Mrs Christmas, surely, is aware of the demands of the season.'

'I'm sorry about not being flat,' Stanley said. 'I did get tired of it, though.'

'No need to apologise,' said Mrs Christmas. 'Flat, round, whatever, people must be what shape they wish.'

'So true,' said Mrs Lambchop. 'But will your husband agree?'

'We shall see. Come.' Mrs Christmas rose, and the Lambchops followed her down the hall.

Mrs Christmas knocked on a door. 'Visitors, dear! From America.'

'Send 'em back!' said a deep voice.

'Sir?' Mr Lambchop tried to sound cheerful. 'A few minutes, perhaps? " 'Tis the season to be jolly", eh? We −'

'Bah!' said the voice. 'Go home!'

'What a terrible temper!' Stanley said. 'He doesn't want to meet us at all!'

'I already *have* met him once,' Arthur whispered. 'In a department store.'

'That wasn't the real one, dear,' Mrs Lambchop said.

'Too bad,' said Arthur. 'He was much nicer than this one.'

Sarah stepped forward. 'Poppa? Can you hear me, Poppa?'

'I hear you, all right!' said the deep voice. 'Took the Great Sleigh without permission, didn't you? Rascal!'

'The letter on your wall, Poppa?' Sarah said. 'The Lambchop letter? Well, they're *here*, the whole family! It wasn't easy, Poppa! I went down their chimney and scraped my knee, and then I banged it, the *same* knee, when I –'

'SARAH!' said the voice.

Sarah hushed, and so did everyone else.

'The flat boy, eh?' said the voice. 'Hmmmm . . .'

Mrs Lambchop took a comb from her bag and tidied Arthur's hair. Mr Lambchop straightened Stanley's collar.

'Come in!' said the voice behind the door.

Chapter Four

Sarah's Father

The room was very dark, but it was possible to make out a desk at the far side, and someone seated behind it.

The Lambchops held their breaths. This was perhaps the most famous person in the world!

'Guess what, Poppa?' said Sarah, sounding quite nervous. 'The Lambchops know *names* for our reindeer!'

No answer came.

'Names, Poppa, not just *numbers*! There's Dashes and Frances and –'

'Dasher,' said Stanley, 'Then Dancer, then –'

'*Then* Frances!' cried Sarah. 'Or is it *Prances*? Then –'

'Waste of time, this!' said the figure behind the desk. But then a switch clicked, and lights came on.

The Lambchops stared.

Except for a large TV in one corner and a speaker-box on the desk, the room was much like Mr Lambchop's study at home. There were bookshelves and comfortable chairs. Framed letters, one of them Stanley's, hung behind the desk, along with photographs of Mrs Christmas, Sarah, and elves and reindeer, singly and in groups.

Sarah's father was large and stout, but otherwise not what they had expected.

He wore a blue zip jacket with 'N. Pole Athletic Club' lettered across it, and sat with his feet, in fuzzy brown slippers, up on the desk. His long white hair and beard were in need of trimming, and the beard had crumbs in it. On the desk, along with his feet, were a plate of cookies, a bowl of potato chips, and a bottle of strawberry soda with a straw in it.

'George Lambchop, sir,' said Mr Lambchop. 'Good evening. May I present my wife Harriet, and our sons Stanley and Arthur?'

'How do you do.' Sarah's father sipped his soda. 'Whichever is Stanley, step forward, please, and turn about.'

Stanley stepped forward and turned about.

'You're *round*, boy!'

'I blew him up,' said Arthur. 'With a bicycle pump.'

Sarah's father raised his eyebrows. 'Very funny. Very funny indeed.' He ate some potato chips. 'Well? What brings you all here?'

Mr Lambchop cleared his throat. 'I understand, Mr – No, that can't be right. What *is* the proper form of address?'

'Depends where you're from. "Santa" is the American way. But I'm known also as Father Christmas, *Père Noel*, *Babbo Natale*, *Julenisse* . . . Little country, way off somewhere, they call me "The Great Hugga Wagoo."'

'Hugga Wagoo?' Arthur laughed loudly,

and Mrs Lambchop shook her head at him.

Mr Lambchop continued, 'We understand, sir – *Santa*, if I may? – that you propose not to make your rounds this year? We are here to ask that you reconsider.'

'Reconsider?' said Sarah's father. 'The way things are these days? Hah! See for yourselves!'

The big TV in the corner clicked on, and he switched from channel to channel.

The first channel showed battleships firing flaming missiles; the second, aeroplanes dropping bombs; the third, cars crashing other cars. Then came buildings burning, people begging for food, people hitting each other, people firing pistols at policemen. The last channel showed a game show, men and women in chicken costumes grabbing for prizes in a pool of mud.

Sarah's father switched off the TV. 'Peace on Earth? Goodwill toward men? Been wasting my time, it seems!'

'You have been watching *far* too much television,' said Mrs Lambchop. 'No wonder you take a dim view of things.'

'Facts are facts, madam! Everywhere, violence and greed! Hah! Right here in my own office, a whole family come begging for Christmas treats!'

The Lambchops were deeply shocked.

'I'm greedy sometimes,' said Stanley. 'But not always.'

'I'm quite nice, actually,' Arthur said. 'And Stanley's even nicer than me.'

'*I*, dear,' said Mrs Lambchop. 'Nicer than I.'

Mr Lambchop, finding it hard to believe that he was at the North Pole having a conversation like this, chose his words with care.

'You misjudge us, sir,' he said. 'There is indeed much violence in the world, and selfishness. But not everyone – we Lambchops, for example –'

'Hah! Different, are you?' Sarah's father spoke into the little box on his desk. 'Yo! Elf Ewald?'

'Central Files,' said a voice from the box. 'Ewald here.'

'Ewald,' said Sarah's father. 'Check this year's letters, under "USA." Bring me the "Lambchop" file.'

Chapter Five

The Letters

Elf Ewald had come and gone, leaving behind a large brown folder.

'Not greedy, Lambchops? We shall see!' Sarah's father drew a letter from the folder and read it aloud.

' "Dear Santa, My parents say I can't have a real car until I'm grown up. I want one now. A big red one. Make that two cars, both red." Hah! Hear that? Shameful!'

Mrs Lambchop shook her head. 'I should be interested,' she said, 'to learn who wrote that letter?'

'It is signed − Hmmmm . . . Frederic. Frederic Lampop.'

Stanley laughed. 'Our name's not "Lampop"! And we don't even know any Frederics!'

'Mistakes *do* happen, you know! I get *millions* of letters!' Sarah's father drew from the folder again. 'Ah! This one's from *you*!'

' "Dear Santa," ' he read. ' "I hope you are fine. I need lots of gifts this year. Shoes and socks and shirts and pants and underwear. And big tents. At least a hundred of each would be nice −" A hundred! *There's* greediness!'

'It does seem a bit much, Stanley,' said Mr Lambchop. 'And why tents, for goodness sake?'

'You'll see,' said Stanley.

Sarah's father read on. '". . . of each would be nice. But not delivered to my house. It was on TV about a terrible earthquake in South America where all the houses fell down, and people lost all their clothes and don't have anywhere to live. Please take everything to where the earthquake was. Thank you. Your friend, Stanley Lambchop. PS. I would send my old clothes, but they are mostly from when I was flat and wouldn't fit anybody else."'

'Good for you, Stanley!' said Mrs Lambchop. 'A fine idea, the tents.'

'Hmmmph! One letter, that's all.' Sarah's father chose another letter. 'This one's got jam on it.'

'Excuse me,' said Arthur. 'I was eating a sandwich.'

' "Dear Santa," ' Sarah's father read, ' "I have hung up a pillow case instead of a stocking —" Hah! The old pillow case trick!'

'Wait!' cried Arthur. 'Read the rest!'

' "... instead of a stocking. Please fill this up with chocolate bars, my favourite kind

with nuts. My brother Stanley is writing to you about an earthquake, and how people there need clothes and tents and things. Well, I think they need food too, and little stoves to cook on. So please give them the chocolate bars, and food and stoves. The bars should be the big kind. It doesn't matter about the nuts. Sincerely, Arthur Lambchop."'

Mrs Lambchop gave Arthur a little hug.

'All right, *two* letters,' said Sarah's father. 'But from brothers. Count as one, really.'

He took a last letter from the folder. 'Nice penmanship, this one . . . Mr and Mrs George Lambchop! Now there's a surprise!'

'Well, why *not*?' said Mrs Lambchop.

Mr Lambchop said, 'No harm, eh, just dropping a line?'

Their letter was read.

'"Dear Sir: Perhaps you expect letters from children only, since as people grow older they often begin to doubt that you truly exist. But when our two sons were very small, and asked if you were real, we said "yes". And if they were to ask again now, we would not say "no". We would say that you are not real, of course, for those who do not believe in you, but very real indeed for those who *do*. Our Christmas wish is that you will never have cause to doubt that Stanley and Arthur Lambchop, and their parents, take the latter position. Sincerely, Mr and Mrs George Lambchop, USA."'

Sarah's father thought for a moment. 'Hmmm . . . *Latter* position? Ah? *Do* believe. I see.'

'See, Poppa?' said Sarah. 'No greediness! Not one –'

'Fine letters, Sarah. I agree.' There was sadness in the deep voice now. 'But all, Sarah, from the same family that thought to deceive me with that "flatness" story. Flat indeed!'

Mrs Lambchop gasped. 'Deceive? Oh, no!'

'Round is round, madam.' Sarah's father

shook his head. 'The lad's shape speaks for itself.'

The hearts of all the Lambchops sank within them. Their mission had failed, they thought. For millions and millions of children all over the world, a joyful holiday was lost, perhaps never to come again.

Arthur felt especially bad. It was his fault, he told himself, for thinking of that bicycle pump.

Stanley felt worst of all. If only he hadn't grown tired of being flat, hadn't let Arthur blow him round again! If only there were proof –

And then he remembered something.

'Wait!' he shouted, and stood on tiptoe to whisper in Mrs Lambchop's ear.

'What . . .?' she said. 'I can't – The *what*? Oh! Yes! I had forgotten! Good for you,

Stanley!'

Rummaging in her bag, she found her wallet, from which she drew a photograph. She gave it to Sarah's father.

'Do keep that,' she said. 'We have more at home.'

The snapshot had been taken by Mr Lambchop the day after the big bulletin board fell on Stanley. It showed him, quite flat, sliding under a closed door. Only his

top half was visible, smiling up at the camera. The bottom half was still behind the door.

For a long moment, as Sarah's father studied the picture, no one spoke.

'My apologies, Lambchops,' he said at last. 'Flat he is. *Was*, anyhow. I've half a mind to –' He sighed. 'But those red cars, asking for *two*, that –'

'That was Lam*POP*!' cried Arthur. 'Not –'

'Just teasing, lad!'

Sarah's father had jumped up, a great smile on his face.

'Yo, elves!' he shouted into his speaker phone. 'Prepare to load gifts! Look lively! Tomorrow is Christmas Eve, you know!'

The next moments were joyful indeed.

'Thank you, thank you! . . . Hooray! . . . Hooray! . . . Hooray!' shouted Mr and

Mrs Lambchop, and Stanley and Arthur and Sarah.

Sarah's mother kissed everyone. Mrs Lambchop kissed Sarah's father, and almost fainted when she realised what she had done.

Then Sarah's father asked Stanley to autograph the sliding-under-the-door picture, and when Stanley had written 'All best wishes, S. Lambchop' across the picture, he pinned it to the wall.

'Blew him round, eh?' he said to Arthur. 'Like to have seen that!'

He turned to Sarah. 'Come, my dear! While I freshen up, teach me those reindeer names. Then I will see our visitors safely home!'

Chapter Six

Going Home

A crowd of elves had gathered with Mrs Christmas and Sarah to say goodbye. 'Bless you, Lambchops!' they called. 'Thank goodness you came! . . . Think if you hadn't! . . . Whew! . . . Farewell, farewell!'

In the Great Sleigh, Sarah's father took up the reins. 'Ready, Lambchops?'

He made a fine appearance now, his hair and beard combed, and wearing a smart green cloak and cap. The famous red suit, he had explained, was reserved for delivering gifts.

'Goodbye, everyone!' called Mrs Lamb-chop. 'We will remember you always!'

'You bet!' cried Stanley. 'I'll *never* forget!'

'But you will, dear,' said Mrs Christmas. 'You will *all* forget.'

'Hardly.' Mr Lambchop smiled. 'An evening like this does not slip one's mind.'

'Poppa will see to it, actually,' said Sarah. 'Snow City, all of us here . . . We're supposed to be, you know, sort of a mystery. Isn't that *silly*? I mean, if —'

'Sarah!' her father said. 'We must go.'

The Lambchops looked up at the night sky, still bright with stars, then turned for a last sight of the little red-roofed house behind them, and of the elves' cottages

about the snowy square.

'We are ready,' said Mr Lambchop.

'Goodbye, goodbye!' called Mrs Lambchop and Stanley and Arthur.

'Goodbye, goodbye!' called the elves,
waving.

The eight reindeer tossed their heads,
jingling their harness bells. One bell flew
off, and Stanley caught the little silver cup
in his hand. Suddenly, as before, the
jingling stopped, all was silence, and the

pale mist rose again about the sleigh.

Sarah's father's voice rang clear. 'Come, Dasher, Dancer, Prancer, Vixen! Come, Comet, Cupid, Donder and . . . oh, whatsisname?'

'Blitzen!' Stanley called.

'Thank you. Come, Blitzen!'

The mist swirled, closing upon the sleigh.

Chapter Seven

Christmas

The Lambchops all remarked the next morning on how soundly they had slept, and how late. Mr Lambchop ate breakfast in a rush.

'Will you be all day at the office, George?' Mrs Lambchop asked. 'It *is* Christmas Eve, you know.'

'There is much to do,' said Mr Lambchop. 'I will be kept late, I'm afraid.'

But there was little to occupy him at his office, since a practical joker had left word he would not be in. He was home by noon to join friends and family for carol singing about the neighbourhood.

Mrs Lambchop had the carolers in for hot chocolate, which was greatly admired. She had added cinnamon, she explained; the idea had just popped into her head. The carolers were all very jolly, and Frank Smith, who lived next door, made everyone laugh, the Lambchops hardest of all, by claiming he had seen reindeer on their lawn the night before.

On Christmas morning, they opened their gifts to each other, and gifts from relatives and friends. Then came a surprise for Stanley and Arthur. Mr Lambchop had just turned on the TV news.

'. . . and now a flash from South America, from where the earthquake was,' the announcer was saying. 'Homeless villagers here are giving thanks this morning for a tremendous supply of socks, shirts, underwear, and food. They have also received a *thousand* tents, and a *thousand* little stoves to cook on!' The screen showed a homeless villager, looking grateful. 'The tents, and the little stoves,' the villager said. 'Just what we need! Bless whoever sends these tents and stoves! Also the many tasty chocolate bars with nuts!'

'He's blessing *me*!' cried Stanley. 'I asked for tents in my letter. But I wasn't sure it would work.'

'Well, *I* wrote about stoves,' Arthur said. '*And* chocolate bars. But they didn't have to have nuts.'

Happy coincidences! thought Mr and Mrs Lambchop, smiling at each other.

Christmas dinner, shared with various aunts, uncles, and cousins, was an enormous meal of turkey, yams, and three kinds of pie. Then everyone went ice-skating in the park. By bedtime, Stanley and Arthur were more than ready for sleep.

'A fine holiday,' said Mr Lambchop, tucking Arthur in.

'Yes indeed.' Mrs Lambchop tucked in Stanley. 'Pleasant dreams, boys, and – What's this?' She had found something on the table by his bed. 'Why, it's a little bell! A silver bell!'

'It was in my pocket,' Stanley said. 'I don't know what it's from.'

'Pretty. Goodnight, you two,' said Mrs

Lambchop, and switched off the light.

The brothers lay silent for a moment in the dark.

'Stanley . . .?' Arthur said. 'It *was* a nice holiday, don't you think.'

'*Extra* nice,' said Stanley. 'But why? It's as if I have something wonderful to remember, but can't think what.'

'Me too. Merry Christmas, Stanley.'

'Merry Christmas, Arthur,' said Stanley, and soon they were both asleep.

Stanley is back, and he's flat – again!
Even his brother Arthur can't come up with
a plan to re-inflate Stanley this time.

But there's fun to be had being flat.
Stanley helps win a boat race and rescues
a girl from a dangerous building.

Heroes come in all shapes and sizes!

STANLEY, FLAT AGAIN!

by Jeff Brown

Pictures by Scott Nash

EGMONT PRESS: ETHICAL PUBLISHING

Egmont Press is about turning writers into successful authors and children into passionate readers – producing books that enrich and entertain. As a responsible children's publisher, we go even further, considering the world in which our consumers are growing up.

Safety First
Naturally, all of our books meet legal safety requirements. But we go further than this; every book with play value is tested to the highest standards – if it fails, it's back to the drawing-board.

Made Fairly
We are working to ensure that the workers involved in our supply chain – the people that make our books – are treated with fairness and respect.

Responsible Forestry
We are committed to ensuring all our papers come from environmentally and socially responsible forest sources.

For more information, please visit our website at
www.egmont.co.uk/ethicalpublishing